Alien Adventures

Goal!

Alison Hawes • **Jonatronix**

OXFORD
UNIVERSITY PRESS

D1470755

Tiger

Cat

Cat and Tiger were kicking a football.

Nok was too little to join in.
"I have a plan," said Max.

Max, Cat and Tiger shrank.

"Now we can all join in," said Max.
"Can I be goalkeeper?" said Nok.

Cat hit the ball between
the flowerpots.
"One goal to me!" she said.

Next, Tiger took a shot. It went past Nok.
"Goal!" Tiger said.

Then, Max ran up to the ball and struck it hard.

Nok put his arms out but the ball hit him in the chest.

He shot back and landed in the web.
"Are you hurt?" said Cat.
"No, just stuck," Nok said.

Just then, a spider crept out from
the flowerpot. Nok was afraid.
"Help!" he said.

The spider crept nearer.
Max held on to Nok's hand and
began to pull.

The children kept on pulling.
At last Nok sprang free.

Nok did a flip. Nok did a kick.

The ball hit the web.
"What a goal!" said Cat.

Goal!

Retell the story

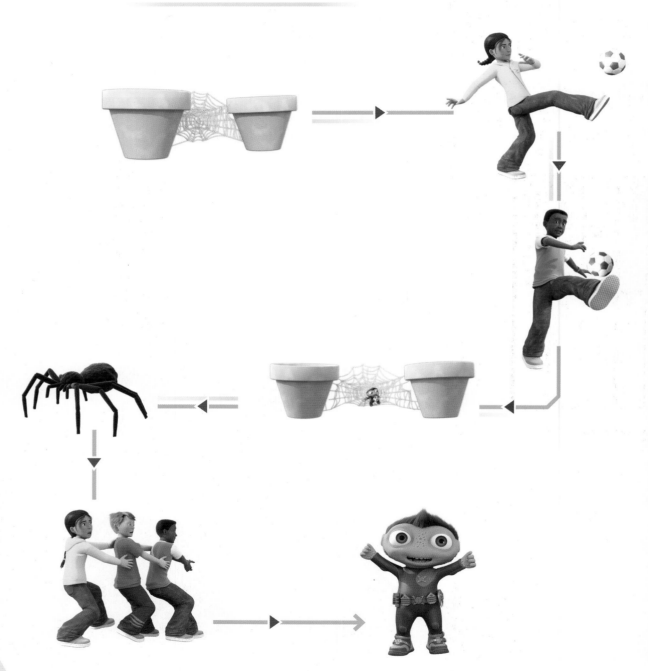